For the other Hedgehog, and my Mouse.

With lots of love.

CJ

little bee books

An imprint of Bonnier Publishing Group

853 Broadway, New York, New York 10003

Text and illustrations copyright © 2015 by Cate James.

First published in Great Britain in 2015 by words & pictures,

an imprint of Quarto Publishing Plc.

This little bee books edition, 2015.

Manufactured in China

First Edition 2 4 6 8 10 9 7 5 3 1

Library of Congress Control Number: 2015935126

ISBN 978-1-4998-0171-2

www.littlebeebooks.com

www.bonnierpublishing.com

Go Home, Little One!

Cate James

little bee books

Florence and Mrs. Hedgehog lived in the
bottom of a tall tree, deep in the forest.
    The squirrel twins, Harry and Barry,
lived upstairs.
    It was almost winter, and some animals
were getting ready for their long winter sleep.

Florence loved spring . . .

Florence loved summer . . .

and Florence loved fall.

But she didn't know if she loved winter, because she always slept right through it.

"I want to stay awake to play in the snow with Harry and Barry," she told Mrs. Hedgehog, who was busy making a feast to enjoy before their winter sleep.

"You can play with Harry and Barry for a little while," said Mrs. Hedgehog, "but don't go too far. We have to get ready to hibernate."

So Florence ran outside to play
hide-and-seek with the squirrel twins.

The three friends
scampered deep
into the forest.

"Hello, little ones! What are you doing out here?"
Mrs. Rabbit asked Florence. "It's going to snow soon.
You should head home."

But Florence and the twins were having
way too much fun to go home.
They skipped even deeper into the forest.
Sure enough, it began to snow.
Florence loved the soft, white snow, even though
it was cold enough to make her toes tingle.

The three friends built
a huge snow-squirrel.
"It's getting dark, little ones,"
said Mr. Badger. "You should
head home."

But the three friends were still
having way too much fun to go home.

All of a sudden, it was dark. Florence started to feel scared. Even the squirrel twins had never been this far away from home before. The sky was full of snow, and Florence couldn't feel her toes now!

"Go home, little ones!" hooted Mr. Owl.
"There's danger in these trees. Be careful!"

"N-Not yet!" said Florence, feeling a
little unsure. She wasn't having so
much fun anymore.

"Hello, little ones!" said Mr. Fox, showing his pointy teeth. "It's time to eat!"

"I WANT TO GO HOME!"

cried Florence at last.

"So do we!" cried Harry and Barry.

Florence and Harry and Barry
ran and ran and ran.

"Help, Mr. Fox is chasing us!"
they said to Mr. Owl.
"I'll distract him!" he hooted.

"Which way is home?"
they asked Mr. Badger.
"Go towards Mrs. Rabbit's house,
it's just over there," he snuffled.

They ran past Mrs. Rabbit's house.
"You're almost there! Go home,
little ones!" she said.

Florence thought this place looked familiar,
but the snow made it hard to tell.
    "What if we can't find our home?" she asked.

But at last, Harry and Barry shouted,
"Look, Florence! It's our tree!"

Mrs. Hedgehog scooped Florence up into a big hug.
"I missed home," Florence said, "and I'm hungry!"

Harry and Barry stayed for the feast, and then it was
time for Florence's winter sleep.

And Florence and Mrs. Hedgehog
slept soundly in their warm tree until spring.